There's an
Alien
IN YOUR BOOK

Written by TOM FLETCHER

Illustrated by GREG ABBOTT

PUFFIN

For Max – T.F.

For Annika – G.A.

PUFFIN BOOKS

UK | USA | Canada | Ireland | Australia | India | New Zealand | South Africa

Puffin Books is part of the Penguin Random House group of companies whose
addresses can be found at global.penguinrandomhouse.com.

www.penguin.co.uk
www.puffin.co.uk
www.ladybird.co.uk

Penguin
Random House
UK

First published 2019
This edition published 2020

001

Copyright © Tom Fletcher, 2019
Illustrated by Greg Abbott

The moral right of the author has been asserted

Printed in China

A CIP catalogue record for this book is available from the British Library

ISBN: 978–0–241–35721–7

All correspondence to:
Puffin Books, Penguin Random House Children's, 80 Strand, London WC2R 0RL

MIX
Paper from
responsible sources
FSC® C018179

OH NO!
A spaceship has crash-landed in your book!

What a lot of smoke!
I think there's something there . . .

Blow the smoke away
and turn the page . . .

AAAARGH! It's an ALIEN!

Look at that big round head . . . yuck!

And those wibbly-wobbly antennae . . . double yuck!

And all those slimy suckers . . .
yuck, yuck, **Yuck!**

Make your scariest face and shout . . .
Go away, Alien!

OH NO!

It's crying . . .
Perhaps we shouldn't have been so mean.

Pat the alien's head to make it feel better.

That's better – look, it's smiling!
(I don't know what it's saying, though – do you?)

aa-zee-zoe!!

Now we need to help Alien get back
up into space. But . . .

We'll have to find another way.

JIGGLE the book UP and DOWN –
that might bounce it back into space . . .

Wow! You bounced Alien high,
but not high enough.

Try **TURNING** the book upside down . . .

Good – now turn the page.
Maybe this will get Alien back
up into space!

Look! Alien is standing on its head –
but it's not in space!

Try **LIFTING** the book **HIGH** up
in the air and turn the page . . .

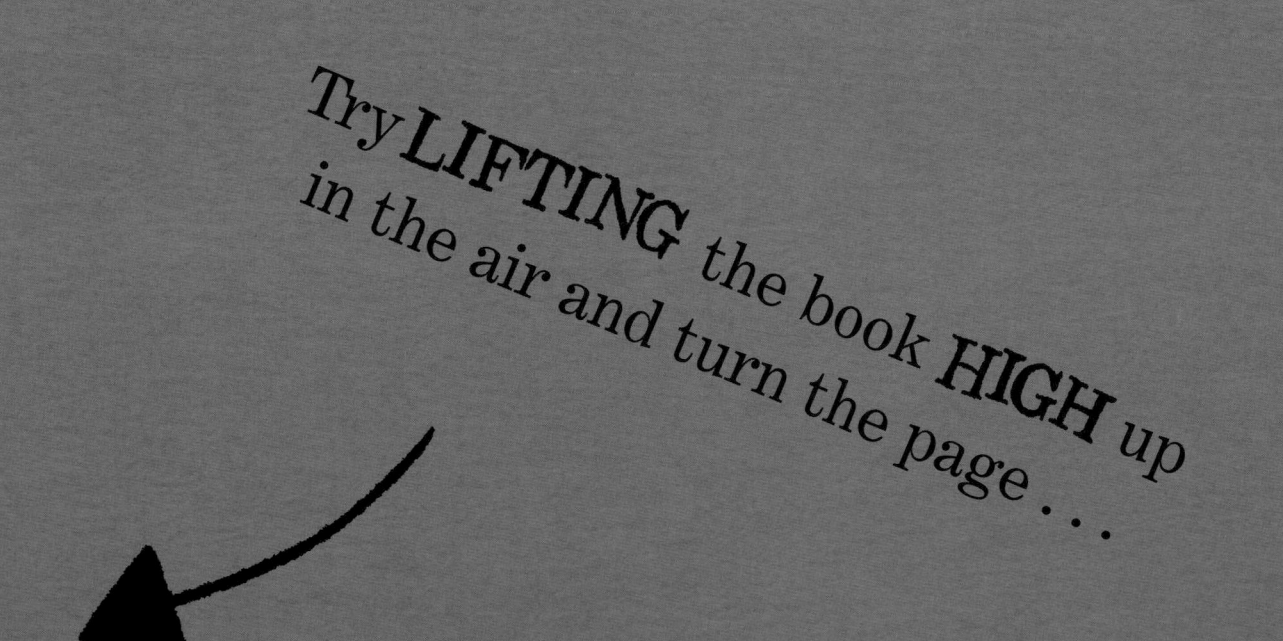

UH-OH!

Alien's very high up,
but it's STILL not in space –
and it looks a little scared . . .

Phew!

Alien's safe
back on the
ground.

But aliens don't belong on Earth – they're
much too different.

Earth is for people . . . and pugs . . .
frogs and bugs,
fish and snails,
bees and whales!

Close your eyes and **IMAGINE** these creatures
to show Alien why it doesn't belong here.

Hang on –
     all those things look pretty different too!

Alien, you've got boggly eyeballs,
wibbly-wobbly antennae
and skin sloppier than a slug, but . . .

we're **all** weird and wonderful . . .

So you're welcome to stay here on Planet Earth!

Now, if Alien is going to stay,
I think it needs a home in this book.

Use your finger to draw a house shape here,
then close your eyes, say **zaa-zee-zoo**,
and turn the page . . .

That looks like the

perfect

home!

Hmm – I think Alien needs a friend to play with.

Shout ...

Come and be friends with Alien!
as loudly as you can.

Well done! It worked!
You called a friendly little monster.

I think he'll make a great friend for Alien
– don't you?

And Monster has a surprise for Alien . . .

He's fixed the spaceship!
Now they are ready for an . . .

ADVENTURE!!

Press the button on the spaceship and count down – 5, 4, 3, 2, 1 . . .

LIFT OFF!
Wave goodbye to Alien and Monster and say . . .

zaa-zee-zoo!